Cinnabar Nocturne

Tiana Or-Gordon

Published by Or-Gordon Enav – Linterin Books

2020

First Edition

10 9 8 7 6 5 4 3 2 1

Edited by Jennifer Paul

Cover painting and graphic design by Vlada Shamova

Printed by Kindle Direct Publishing, an Amazon.com Company

Available from www.Amazon.com

(First Printing)

ISBN: 978-80-907066-4-4

First Online Publishing:

ISBN: 978-80-907066-3-7 (Kindle eBook)

CINNABAR NOCTURNE

CINNABAR NOCTURNE

FOR ERVIN

CONTENTS

DANCE

She entered the forest as the sun began to sink into the horizon, to spill into the pink cotton clouds that seemed to be dotted with glittering, sticky sugar, as it left her little spot of Earth in order to proceed in its never-ending quest toward its last, freshest, newest step, marked by a shining golden footprint, far away behind the thin tree bark, behind their scratched surface, their long shadows that keep stretching as the sun slowly disappears, trying desperately to catch a beam of attention to light the trees during the night, but they never succeed, only try again and again, stretching thin fingers over the dry leaves on the ground, and then crawling back to their trees with the darkness of the night, which caresses the branches, hushes the chiming leaves, envelops the bark with a dim whisper without words, singing the rocking song of night, letting the notes slide like raindrops from the invisible velvety sky onto the ever-growing evergreen needles and then down the peeling red crust, sliding on and on into the wet mossy ground, into the smell of rain and tears, climbing down the steady roots forever and ever, ringing the melody in the eternal darkness as the roots make their way through the Earth, groping, searching, twisting for the unknown, for the hidden treasure of existence, for the unknown meaning of their route, until the notes stick to their slow restlessness and let only a silent echo return through the path already discovered up and up, back toward the rustling surface of the woods and to the fading twilight, following its trace to and fro on the dry leaves and through fallen petals, echoing a laughter it had heard in a distant dream, running, rolling until it encounters her bare toes and follows their slightest moves, the sweat on her feet, the dirt beneath her nails, the regular swing of her ankle each time she raised her foot to step a little farther, the bending of her knees, the muscles stiffening in her thighs, the rotation of her hips, the tension in her waist, the air's circulation inside her lungs, the beating of her heart creating rhythm for her entire body, her focused gaze, her dilated pupils and the last glistening strings of light they managed to swallow, all this does the silent echo of the sounds see and hear and feel before it hurries back down the moving legs toward its original notes that had stayed in the ground, buried amongst the sleeping shadows, but then the echo slows down as her movement does, as she prepares to stop walking for three beats, the echo hears the first and breaks into a million tiny echoes of a charming song, soaking into her skin like drops of sea foam, rolling down the hill out of the forest until they reach a deep river and join the way of countless drops on their passage to the mythical calmness of the sea, where she suddenly notices the touch of the song's echo and the silent song itself surrounding her, where she let her eyes close and her mind merge with the still air, where she followed the sun, and the shadows, and the night melody, and the tree roots, and the river in a never-ending, everlasting dance.

ALEX

A noise woke me up. It was dull, yet sudden. I tried to look around and could see nothing but the thick darkness. I felt like a bug inside an ink bottle, whose eyes soaked up the poisonous black liquid, huge amounts of it, in a desperate struggle to clear a tiny tunnel that would give way to the light on the other side. Outside. Still, reason reminded me that there was no light outside. The sky was cloudy during the afternoon; the clouds must have blocked the luminous night sky.

I waited motionless. The noise came again. It sounded like a single knock coming from the window on the wall behind me. *Alex!*

Without realizing my mistake, I jumped out of bed, the floor squeaking loudly. I shivered. Not because the air was cold, it wasn't. It was just…chilly. I heard the sheets rustle from the other side of the room as Al moved in his sleep. I must have disturbed him. I bit my lower lip, facing the task I had to undertake. I had to find my bed again. With my arms stretched before me, and in tiny hesitant steps, I started crossing the room. When my knee finally hit something low and hard, which under the circumstances could be called a bed frame, another sigh revealed that it was Al's bed, and that I had been following the wrong direction.

It took me forever to wade through the darkness back to my bed and then find the little table next to it. *Careful, careful…* I thought as I patted the table's surface. At last I found them. Relieved, I put my glasses on. The room seemed immediately brighter, and I could spot the third stone as it hit the window.

I exited, crossed the corridor in two steps, and ran down the six stairs to the ground floor. Without stopping, I opened the wooden door and found myself outside.

Alex was standing there with his arms crossed on his chest. "What took you so long?" he scorned.

"I had to find my glasses," I defended myself.

"You took them off? You fell asleep!? What kind of a man are you?"

"I was tired," I shrugged.

He rolled his eyes but started walking. I cast one more glance at the wooden hut and ran to catch him.

"Why did you want to get up anyway?" I asked as we were crossing the wet lawn.

"I heard it was ready," he smiled whimsically.

"What?"

"Honeycomb."

I stopped. "The beehive is on the other side of the grounds!"

"So what? The grounds aren't that big anyway."

I didn't move, angry that he made me get up in the middle of the night.

"Come on, Alex, it'll be fun!"

I grumbled but walked on. The grounds consisted of five dormitories (those tiny wooden huts), a dining hall, also wooden, a swimming pool, a camp fire, and a beehive. There was also supposed to be a theater, but no one knew where to find it. It was a summer camp of sorts, except we never saw the owner, the organizer of the place. The other strange thing was that we all had the same name. Fifty children, boys and girls alike, of all ages and all nationalities bearing the same name. It wasn't intentional, we checked, and the employees were just as surprised as we were. Not that they had anything to do with us, they just looked after the buildings and the gardens; we were free to do as we chose. There were, however, two rules we had to respect: going to bed at eleven, and not sharing a room with a girl. Not that the little ones cared, but we fifteen-year-olds were a little disappointed.

We walked for a long time. The minutes seemed to stretch themselves over all their endless nanoseconds with no intention of allowing us to pass. Except for the grass squeaking beneath our feet, everything was quiet. A tall street lamp lit our path now and then. It looked quite funny, because there was no street.

"Why today?" I whispered at last.

"I heard the guy who takes care of the bees talking with some kid. He said they're full of the perfect honey. It's their time of year."

"There's always honeycomb in the beehive!"

"Yeah, but now it's the best honeycomb."

We continued walking. Then I asked, "Why didn't you just ask the guy to give you some?"

"He said he wouldn't. It's for sale."

"Why didn't you buy it?"

Alex stopped, giving me a look of derision. "And spend so much on honey? You out of your mind?"

I shrugged. "Less trouble than stealing it."

"But also less fun."

Finally, I could spot the beehive in the distance. It was a collection of IKEA-like boxes that made a loud, buzzing sound. The sound always made me nervous; it reminded me of the time I got stung and discovered I was allergic. Since then I've kept my distance from bees and wasps alike, but there was no trace of the buzzing sound tonight. This made me even more nervous. And very excited. Al was right. Stealing is really fun.

Stealing is disrespecting others. Pushing boundaries. Feeling your heart beating in your throat. Feeling alive. Feeling human.

We slowed our pace as we got closer and started walking amongst the boxes. Suddenly Alex lifted one's lid.

"Alex!" It was strange, using my name for somebody else. I felt as if I was scolding myself, holding myself back. I didn't want to hold myself back, it didn't make sense. A quiet buzz drifted into the night sky from the open beehive, hinting at pain and fear.

"Quickly," I spat.

Alex's hand dove into the box. It remained there.

"Come on!"

The buzz grew louder, a few bees flew out. A dog barked somewhere nearby. Its barking became louder and louder, as did the buzzing of the bees, until the animal emerged from behind the beehive, running straight toward us. Only at that moment did my companion turn back and run.

We ran through the beehives, we ran across the grass, past the huts, the dining hall, climbed over the chairs and benches around the fireplace, turning and changing our direction to confuse our pursuer. The dog continued barking behind us. Just as his panting almost reached us, we saw the gate. We gathered our strength, we ran faster, feeling the chilly air sliding past our cheeks, then caught the iron loops of the gate, and climbed. When we were high enough, we flung ourselves to the other side. The dog stayed behind, trapped.

Immediately, we forced ourselves to get up from the damp ground and run into the bushes, in fear of encountering the grown-ups. A gurgling laugh escaped us now and then between our heavy breaths.

As soon as we entered the shrubs, we collapsed and fell onto the cold grass, laughing hysterically.

"Show…show me the spoils," I panted.

Alex opened his jacket and took out a raggedly wrapped piece of sponge. He waved with it victoriously.

"That's it?" I couldn't help feeling disappointed.

"What's wrong with it?"

"Well… for starters, it's really small," I said.

Alex looked at the sponge hesitantly. "We couldn't take the whole sheet. It's too big."

"Why not?"

"It's too big!" he repeated, obviously annoyed by my attitude.

"What if we took a bad part?"

"What do you mean, 'bad part'?"

"A less tasty part?"

"It's the good time of year, all the parts are tasty."

"What if the other parts are better?"

He thought for a while. "Then we'll take another part of the honeycomb tomorrow." Alex tore the sponge in two and handed me the part in his left hand.

"See, now I get to taste one small part and I won't ever know whether your part was better."

"I'll tell you."

"But how can you know whether or not yours was better than mine if you hadn't tried mine?"

Alex sighed. "We'll switch in the middle. That way we'll taste both."

"But one half of my part will surely taste a little different than the other!"

"What do you want me to do, Alex?" he shouted.

"Examine the whole honeycomb!"

"We don't have the whole honeycomb!"

We sat there, in front of each other, angry with each other.

"Every little part can be really different," I repeated at last.

"They're all the same!" he puffed, and held the honeycomb close to my glasses, "Hexagons, see? That's the whole point of hexagons! They're all the same!"

I shook my head. "They just seem the same. Like… for example…we're all named Alex, does that mean we're just the same?"

"That's a completely different thing." He crossed his arms and looked away. "Are you gonna eat that or not?" he asked at last.

Without arguing, I put my part of the honeycomb in my mouth. Whole. My friend took his time and ate in bites. We'd chew noisily for a long while and then we'd spit out the wax.

Thin, faint stripes of pink and orange crossed the dark night sky from above the clouds. Without exchanging a word, we threw the wax into the bushes and climbed over the fence again. We had to return to bed before anyone realized we were gone. As we crossed the lawn hastily, we slowed in front of the girls' hut. I stopped altogether.

"There's this one girl," I said quietly, "with really dark hair."

"I know," he replied, "and I bet she knows, too. You shouldn't let everyone see how you blush when she passes by."

I gazed at my feet and felt the red smudges crawling on my ears.

"I think she's seventeen."

"Did you know she plays the harp?"

***

I awoke just as the morning lights started coloring the clouds. It was not yet five a.m., but I sat up anyway. I spent most of the night waking up and the rest of it in a troubled sleep. Today was the day. The big day. The day of the concert.

I was in charge of it-- of the organization, performance, and timing. I oversaw the auditions of the performers and rehearsed with them for hours and hours every day. I planned the choreography in the evenings and dreamed about it at night. Everything had to be perfect. Today I had time to prepare the room itself and make some final preparations. The guests would arrive around six. I had more than twelve hours.

As I leaned to pick up my bottle of water, I happened to glance outside. There were two boys standing on the lawn, talking. They were not a part of the show; therefore, I failed to recognize them, but I couldn't help wondering what kept them up. Were they nervous? Excited? Awaiting someone? I had a feeling some of the parents would come to see our performance this evening.

As unnerving as this whole experience may have appeared, I enjoyed it very much and thought of it as a high honor. The owner himself had sent me a very official email asking me to organize it.

"You are a gifted musician and natural leader," it said.

The show consisted of various performances, most of them musical. The most important was the one to come last, where I played the Celtic harp, accompanied by the drums and wooden flutes of all the other young performers. It was my first time playing the Celtic harp in public, and sweat covered my fingers every time I thought of it.

Yet the number I was most proud of was a play showing the life of Alexander the Great using famous dramatic monologues, as well as music. The project was my idea. I thought it could be relevant, as we all bore his name, or at least a variation of it. During the afternoons spent over history textbooks and internet articles, I have come to admire this man, who managed to conquer the entire world known to his culture. This man was loved, feared, and despised by his peers; this man had so many faces, so many personalities. With each conquered inch, with each lost stable of grass, another new personality would emerge and become a part of Alexander the Great, of this perfect whole.

Carefully, so that I wouldn't wake Al who was still asleep in her bed, I got up and walked toward the wardrobe. I took out the dress I saved especially for this day.

The look of it confused me. It was gray and dwindling, lifeless. This wasn't the way it looked before. It used to be... I forgot which color. The fabric had seemed glistening and thick, now it reminded me of a dry petal. My shoulders seemed unusually pale as I put it on, and lean, almost ill. I hurried to find my lipstick. The dark red lips added some color to my face, but it was rather obvious it was unnatural.

Just as I was about to open the door and exit, Alex sighed. I looked back. She opened her brown eyes and blinked a couple of times before sitting up.

"Is it tomorrow?" she yawned.

"It's today," I answered, my heart fluttering in my chest.

"Oh," said Alex and yawned again, "so tomorrow became today. And today became yesterday."

I nodded.

"It's basically the same thing."

Except today we have a concert, I thought and entered the corridor. Most of the girls liked sleeping with the door open and as I walked down the hall, I saw them rising one by one. I went down the stairs. The sky outside seemed a little brighter when I reached the ground floor.

Only outside did I remember that I didn't know where the theater was. I was told not to look for it before the day of the show, and I didn't. Now I had to find it.

The boys I had seen earlier were already gone and the camp was asleep. I decided the most effective way to spot the theater was to walk around and pass all the buildings until I found it. I started walking, my eyes fixed on the huts on my left. The windows were big and clean, and with each step I saw another person waking, sitting up in bed, stretching and yawning, rubbing their eyes. Boys and girls. Children, teenagers, even middle aged and old people. Tall and short. Slim and sturdy. Energetic and tired. Laughing, crying, frowning, or smiling. Diving into the new day or waiting behind in order to understand a confused dream. All awake. All named Alex.

I found myself back in front of my dormitory. I walked around the entire camp without seeing the theater. I started walking again, following my previous steps.

Some of those I woke earlier were now outside, heading toward the dining hall, or simply standing and soaking in the morning air. I moved slower now, focusing on the buildings rather than on the people, but no theater was to be seen. All the buildings were already familiar to me. Could the one I was looking for be somewhere else?

Unreasonable fear seized me, as it often did when I was unsure of my actions, and I continued walking in circles, the wind playing with my dark hair and colorless dress. As I paced around, more and more people came out of the huts. For no reason I gradually started counting as they emerged outside, perhaps to calm myself down, as children do with imaginary sheep before they fall asleep.

Twenty…twenty-six…thirty-one…forty-four…forty-seven…forty-nine…fifty.

Suddenly the hut I was just passing by caught my attention. It bore a sign I hadn't noticed before.

Theater

Getting to know Alex

I stopped, astonished. Was the sign there all along? I looked at the hut itself. It was the very same dormitory I had been staying in since I arrived! I was also puzzled by the sentence below. Did someone add it to the sign? Did someone think the show was too personal, that it revealed too much about me? Did I get carried away while planning it? I shook my head. This couldn't be right, why would anybody do such a strange thing? Besides, I remembered, I was not the only Alex here; the strange comment could refer to anyone!

With a smile of relief, I entered the hut, whose door was already open, and followed the guiding signs with gratitude. All were properly illuminated and visible, and I started imagining the stage itself, biting my nails to camouflage my excitement. I was led to a winding stairway that swept me down, into the ground. The air became heavy, the walls were wet, the stairs slippery. There was no handrail, and the walls on my sides would just make me lose my balance. I slowed, gazing at my feet, moving one only after making sure the other was safely placed on the lower step.

All of a sudden, the dampness in the still air disappeared entirely, to be replaced by the warm odor of sweat. So this was the theater. I looked around, searching for a sign to welcome me, but none could be seen. Upon turning back to the stairs, wishing to return and get my harp and notes, I found only a bare wall.

"All right," I said out loud, even though my voice trembled a little, "I shall take a look at the theater first."

I passed through a gate that stood, yawning, before me, crossed a tiny round hall, with walls and floor gray as cement, passed through another, smaller gate, crossed a somewhat larger hall, and encountered a third gate. "Is this a theater?" I asked. For no reason, I suddenly worried that I managed to insult someone with this comment, perhaps the walls themselves, and so I added, "It is certainly very unique." I passed more and more rooms, each bigger than its predecessors, and walked through gates that gradually shrank. I started panting, my legs trembled with effort, and when I raised my hand to bite my fingernails, I saw that it was frail and scarred with wrinkles. "It must be the light confusing me," I calmed myself.

At last, I reached a gate half my size. When I tried to lean forward and pass through, pain burned my whole body and I sat down, exhausted. Upon taking a second look, my ankles seemed shrunken, too, and were now helplessly lying in my silky high heel shoes. I winced. Without getting up, I pushed myself through the gate, breathing heavily. Another descending stairway awaited me on the other side. I took my shoes off, forced myself to get up, and followed them, one by one, slowly and hesitantly, like a little child.

After ages of climbing down the steps, I entered a room wrapped in black curtains and with a large entrance to another, similar room.

"This must be the backstage!" I cried, with a hint of renewed energy.

Both rooms were enormous and empty, smelling like the sweat that now covered me entirely. The echo of my bare feet hitting the floor vaporized into it as well. A frameless mirror was hung on the wall in the second room, on the wall opposite to the curtains dividing it from the stage. I peeked at my reflection, but froze as I saw it.

My eyes had a terrified look, and they were surrounded by deep wrinkles, wrinkles of stress, wrinkles of worry. The eyelashes were almost gone and the eyebrows very thin. The lips were dry and colorless, and my dark hair was striped with white. My dress hung upon my lean, bent figure like crumpled origami paper.

What happened? I failed to breathe. I wanted to touch my hair, rip out the white, alien stripes. They belonged to someone else. But all I managed to do was take out my red lipstick again, and color my lips.

"The show must go on," I told the room coldly. I stepped toward the curtains, grabbed one in each hand, and pushed them aside. Darkness filled the sky. The stage was but a wooden semicircle on the ground, surrounded by lines of chairs that grew longer and longer, standing one behind the other with no visible end. All were full of people and their impatient hum flew above the seats.

I gasped. I closed the curtains, turning around abruptly. The room was suddenly full of children, instruments, papers, costumes, and a buzzing sound of general excitement. The show was about to begin.

I started running in panic, looking desperately for my harp. How could such a thing happen to me? I planned everything to the last detail, and suddenly everything took place without me. There were many harps. Too many harps. Some were old, some were modern, some had flowers, birds, or names engraved on them, some were plain and simple, some were mahogany, some were chestnut, some were white, and one was blue. All of them were pedal harps.

Of course I preferred the pedal harp to any other instrument, but tonight I was supposed to play the Celtic harp. I found one, tiny and ridiculous, amongst a pile of musical instruments, but it belonged to someone else.

"I'd love to play the pedal harp," I said, "it's more elegant and more comfortable, and I can play anything on it; I love its sound, but not today. I can't carry it around." I passed by an Erard. "I have to carry it around stage!" I explained helplessly to the walls.

The first bell rang. I felt tears forming in my eyes. I ran back to the backstage. "I still have plenty of time till the last number," I calmed myself.

The second bell rang. All I had to do now was to introduce tonight's show and then disappear quietly until it's time for my song. I cast another glance at the mirror, at my pale, wrinkled, tired, pitiful self.

The third bell rang. I stepped out. Immediately as I entered the darkness on stage, my body straightened, my legs strengthened, and energy filled my veins. I looked at my feet, that were smooth and brown again, touched my hands and face, feeling that the wrinkles were gone. My hair was darker than the sky itself, and my dress glistened in the dim light from above.

A regular rhythm suddenly came from behind me. It was the rhythm of the last song, the one I was supposed to play. Children of all ages stood around me in a semicircle, beating drums and playing flutes, waiting for me to start the melody itself.

I'll sing, I thought, looking desperately for an alternative plan, *my voice is the instrument I always carry with me.*

I smiled confidently, knowing that this was my moment of fame. I opened my mouth and sang.

But the voice that came out of me was not my voice. It sounded like fifty different voices, young and old, clear and hoarse, high and low. The words that came out of me were not my words. They just passed through me, from the past into the listeners' future.

Maybe all men got one big soul ever'body's a part of.

Maybe we're all just one person, glued together with honey.

Maybe we're all just hexagons

in a torn up honeycomb.

YOU & ME

"Where are you? Who's with you?"
"Nobody. Me, myself and I."
- J.D. Salinger, The Catcher in the Rye

It was there that I first saw him. The double. The daring fraud. Wrapped in a sickly yellow robe, his hair braided, an overly shiny necklace high above the tips of the fabric.

I sneered. If they wished to irritate me they would have to try harder. This attempt was simply pathetic. And yet I fidgeted a little while looking around the box. The features of my neighbors seceded from the darkness shortly after the twisted golden ornaments that climbed up and down the crimson walls. They did not seem to distinguish the absurd parody from the rest of the play. Ridiculous as it was, I could not help feeling a wave of relief. Fake letters, uninvited houseguests, and phony phone calls were one thing, but a publicly displayed living caricature crossed the line.

I will find the fraud and have a talk with him when Juliet dies, I decided.

As we descended to the buffet, still adjusting to the bright light reflected by the large gilded mirrors, and penetrated into the silk-clad crowd, one of the young girls with whom I shared the box asked, "Who was the lady in yellow? I do not recall such a role in the play, and she had no lines."

"It's supposed to be a parody," I explained politely, "they tend to pull tricks like that."

"Oh!" she, or one of the others, exclaimed. Or one of the

men that joined us on the way, whose lacquer shoes clapped along the stairway. It didn't really matter.

I purchased a glossy little packet of chocolate-covered almonds and approached the nearest table, around which already stood a group of shimmering people. I was surrounded by the conversation almost immediately.

"Do you agree, dear?"

"In my opinion, the scenery is just marvelous. So much better than in the production last October," I replied, taking my white gloves off.

"The contrast between light and shade reflects the war between the families as well as the inner struggle within the characters themselves," nodded a bearded man on my right.

"Which perfectly illustrates *'to be or not to be?'*. What a monologue!"

The cashews were rather bitter, but I didn't really mind. They were only a part of the general atmosphere.

The door opened numerous times as I slicked my long gold evening dress in front of the mirror back in my loge. The newcomers started a quiet conversation or exchanged pleasant smiles with those in the boxes in front of us. It was not until the third bell that I assumed my seat. The ill-conceived caricature did not reappear on stage, yet I did cast a glance at my co-viewers. The young men seemed to take an unusual interest in the predetermined plot.

A dozen warm smiles and sweaty handshakes greeted me in the backstage, and the muffled laughter mixed with my compliments. "Wonderful! What an excellent cast! What costumes!"

The director's pride shone on his flushed, lively cheeks.

"Where is the dear lady who played the extra part?" I asked with delightful amazement upon smiling at the worn out actors.

"Which lady?"

"With the yellow garment."

We looked about the room. The person I was looking for was not present.

"Why, she must have left already, or perhaps she is in the dressing room. Would you mind waiting for a brief moment? I assure you we will find her; she'll be pleased by your valuable interest…"

"Oh, please, it is all right," I raised my hand a little, "do not worry because of me. Besides, I should not be keeping you from your well deserved rest any longer."

"No, it's no trouble. Is there any way I can help you, miss?"

"No, no, just give my best to everyone."

"I certainly will."

I let him kiss the back of my hand, which quite disappeared between his two gentle palms, before wearing my black gloves and departing.

In spite of the many offers, I took a cab; I preferred to be alone. The streets were significantly emptied by the night, even though it was not yet half past eleven. Shortly afterwards, the glass skyscraper emerged in front of us.

A loud beep pierced the air while I put the chip on the scanner. The large door gave way and my hand immediately reached for the light switch. LED brightness filled the space like water pouring into a pot. In the depths of this shadowless light the darkness outside seemed to be expelled miles away. The objects in the room also lost their normal effect; they suddenly seemed detached, unrealistic, or maybe it was all just in my head. I wasted a few long minutes in the elevator, trying to distinguish its quiet noise from the numb silence and looking for wrinkles in my business suit. Finally, I reached my office, sank into one of the leather armchairs and checked the computer for messages. The mailbox was empty. So was my personal email address, social media (private and public), and voicemail. I quickly found the number with which they last called, and waited patiently for the ringing to start.

The phone was answered by a robotic voice. *The number you dialed does not exist. Please try again.*

Of course. I opened my call history and browsed through the unknown received calls. The numbers were random, which made sense as most of them really were customers trying to reach me, but some were the camouflage of the intruders. One by one, I tried all the suspicious numbers. They were either answered by the robot or by the automatic voicemail, because they counted on me dialing back, or because of the late hour. So I went to the kitchen and brought the watering can from beneath the sink. My plants in the office already started to seem artificial.

The elevator's droning noise mixed with the sound of hurrying cars outside. Under normal circumstances I would have ignored it, but being alone, and quite tired, I stuck my fingers into my ears. It didn't help much but at least the buzz was weakened.

The chip wasn't necessary for exiting, so I didn't bother reaching into my handbag. Locking was also an unnecessary precaution.

The tall buildings echoed the clopping of my high heels, flinging the sounds from corner to corner, rolling them down one street and later blowing up the other until I didn't know how many high heels were originally there and where I was exactly.

At last I reached the brownish block near the street corner. The heavy door squeaked as I pushed it open. I groped around, trying to find the wall, and slowly walked forward, where I knew lay the steep stairs. There was definitely someone upstairs, for a dim stripe of light slid down the stairway from the first floor. I followed it, and was surprised to see Betty standing by her desk, rearranging a bundle of papers beneath the old yellow lamp.

"What are you doing here so late?"

She gave a start, but then recognized me and laughed, "You mean so early?"

I glanced at the round clock on the wall behind me. It was four a.m. "So early," I repeated.

"I have this interview today, but I didn't wanna waste a day at work…"

"I see," I said, leaning on her desk, my threadbare jeans rustling.

"And what about you?"

"I don't know… just felt like getting up early."

"Wha'about that fancy job opportunity?"

"Dunno yet, they'll call back."

We were quiet for a while. "Did you already check the messages?" I asked.

"Yeah. Nothing. Do you expect them today?"

"No, it's just that I've been trying to track somebody down."

Betty smiled whimsically. "Jim?"

"No."

"Come on, you can tell me."

"No, some guys that keep pulling practical jokes on me in a desperate attempt to humiliate me."

"Like what?"

"Like…" A figure beneath the blurry window caught my attention. It walked unusually straight and was dressed in torn jeans and a pink sweater, the hair tied in a ponytail, just like me. So they didn't stop this silly imitation. Without another word I hurried down the stairs, rushed through the brightening old lobby, glancing once again at Betty upstairs, who continued sorting her paperwork as if no conversation occurred, and exited.

I caught a glimpse of pink and dark blue before the figure disappeared around the corner.

At this point, I started running.

I ran as fast as I could, using the blowing wind to support me, hitting the bumps and landing in the occasional dents in the sidewalk, spreading my arms to maintain my balance. I didn't think of the streets and corners; I knew the way perfectly. The books and pencils jumped and rattled in my bag. I feared my water bottle might open and wet everything, but I kept running. Just as the bell rang I barged in, exactly in time to join my classmates who already walked down the stairs to the big hall.

"I started thinking you weren't gonna show up," remarked Julia, who automatically started walking by my side, "or that you'd come late."

"I'm never late."

Meanwhile, children of all ages from the other classes headed to the hall as well, blocking the corridor, trying to push their way through.

"Do they really think they can squeeze the entire school into that room?" I complained.

"It's ridiculous," confirmed Julia, "I just hate those assemblies. And those twelve-year-olds, they really can't behave."

I nodded. "No one really, even the grade beneath us, and they're seventeen."

"When are they gonna grow? A little maturity, is that so much to ask?"

We shook our heads and sighed. The children kept squirting out of the classrooms, rushing out of one door, accumulating in front of another, and finally stopping in place before the last one, chatting and yelling, moving restlessly as they tried to pass through. Even though we were the first to enter the corridor, we soon found ourselves pushed to the wall by the countless children.

"This one is so tiny!" someone said as they pointed at a boy that was significantly shorter than the others.

"This one is quite tall."

"This one has pink hair! Who would let a kid dye her hair?"

It became our habit to comment about the little ones when we had nothing better to do.

"Hey, look!" Julia poked at me, "That little girl looks like you!" She pointed at a skinny child in a marshmallow-purple shirt. Her brown hair was divided into two braids and her brown eyes wandered from one corner of the room to the other. Unlike the other children, she was not pushing anyone or fighting for her spot, but instead drifted from side to side with them. Julia was right. There was some likeness in our movements, which were gentle and careful; the big eyes were fairly similar to mine, as were the long black eyelashes.

A growing ball of anger itched at me from the inside. I left my friends and waded in the pool of ever moving children toward the little girl. Most of the midgets did not even reach my hips, yet I was carried away by the streams or lost sight of her numerous times. Finally, she understood that she was the reason for my journey. Her head bowed in silent acceptance, she remained where she was, moving a little because of the passing others, but always returning to the exact same spot, not running away, or trying to ease the effort for me.

I stopped about a meter before her. I looked at her white forehead; she gazed at her feet. The anger that threatened to grow turned into a cool sense of moral obligation.

"Who do you think you are." I said at last.

"Nobody," she peeped.

"What were you thinking."

The little round head bowed further.

"Who else is behind this?"

A little thin finger pointed at me.

"Behind this absurd harassment, you fool."

She shrugged.

Slowly, I kneeled, making her gaze drown into mine. "Listen to me and listen to me well. What you are doing is called identity theft and is a serious crime. I can report you anywhere at any time and get you into a swamp you won't easily escape. You will lose your own little mind in the labyrinth of mine just as your innocent brown stare is being swallowed by mine right now. Learn to value the souls of others before you forever lose yours." With these words I rose, turning back slowly.

The squeaky voice stopped me. "Thank you."

I looked around.

"For what you've said," she added.

Our eyes stayed connected for a few more moments, and then I started walking away, back toward my classmates. Meanwhile, the traffic jam in the entrance to the hall suddenly dissolved and I found myself standing in the middle of rapidly flowing waves of children. My friends near the wall, too, started moving, getting dragged or pushed on and on until the high, narrow door started sucking them in one by one. I gathered my strength, forced the tired muscles in my legs to work harder, but as I put more effort into my moves, the flow passing me grew, and I was swimming against the current.

Exhausted from the effort and a growing, worrying feeling of desperation, of helplessness, my lids fell, and for a while my gaze was lost in my own warm, comforting darkness.

Suddenly the tension enveloping me from all directions

disappeared. The change was so abrupt, so unexpected that I lost my balance altogether. My head felt lighter than ever, my limbs completely slack. I heard, as if from a huge distance, an echo's echo of my body hitting the hard ground, the muffled pain of a new bruise, of the sand pinned on it, pushed against the damaged skin into the sensitive red marks.

Without me commanding it, my body moved carefully, trying to get up, to feel the extent of the injury, to abandon this vulnerable position. The same, sandy ache itched at my right temple, my right cheek, my right shoulder, my right hip.

I opened my eyes, first the left, then the right. A flat landscape unfolded before them, and a gray sky above. The ground was only a few shades darker than the seemingly two-dimensional sky, covered with countless grains of sand, every single one visible, round and coarse. Metal bars sprayed with faded colors of green and red stood here and there, sometimes tied by wrinkled ropes full of dried dust. I sat up, this time by my will, closing my eyes to prevent the sand from entering my vision. Then I wiped my hands in my short puffy skirt and looked again from a higher perspective.

I was sitting in the playground. So near the merry-go-round that if someone stepped on it, it could have hit me at any moment. Except there wasn't anyone on it. Or near it. Or on the swings. Or on the monkey bars. Not even on the other side of the low net fence. The playground was deserted.

Leaning on my left hand, I stood up clumsily, shaking the dust off my skirt and short sleeves. I froze at the sound of steps approaching me. These were not the light quick steps of children racing joyfully to the sandbox. These were the slow, resolute steps of a single person. I jumped on the merry-go-round and stood on my tiptoes so that I could lean my forehead on the railing. Thusly prepared and equipped, I waited.

The steps were aiming toward me. Gradually, they slowed, and when they almost reached the merry-go-round, they stopped altogether. I looked at the newcomer, from her little ballerina shoes up the peach tights, up the pink puffy skirt, until I saw her marshmallow-purple t-shirt, the thin gentle neck, two dark braids, and serious brown eyes. I gasped with a mixture of irritation and disbelief. It was me.

We stood face to face for a long time. Me and my reflection. Her and her reflection. At this moment I knew that I finally caught the double. That daring fraud. But now I wasn't sure whether it was her imitating me, or me imitating her. Or maybe we were both one and the same person. Or maybe we were each a person very different from the other, so reversed, that our twisted minds started thinking that we actually looked alike.

At last I shook my head, shook off those irrational thoughts. I gathered my reason and said to her at last, "You are me."

"You are me," she repeated.

"No, I am who I am and you are trying to steal it."

The double only returned my calm brown stare.

"You are not who you repeatedly try to be. I am the only me."

"How do you know it's not me?" she asked.

"Because it's me."

"How do you know it's you?"

"Because I am me."

"How do you know I am not you?"

"Because if you are me then who am I?"

"Me."

We let the silence rise from the sand to the dense air. I was the one to disturb it, not her.

"If you are me and I am 'me' then what you just said can't be true. One of us isn't."

"If you are me and I am 'me' then one of us is nonexistent."

"Suppose it's you."

"Suppose it's 'me'."

"Which 'me'?"

"I don't know yet."

Very slowly, without taking my eyes off the eyes of the "me" in front of me, I stepped off the merry-go-round, bent down, and took a handful of the coarse sand. Even slower, I stood up again, clutching the grains, until our eyes leveled.

I threw the sand at her chest. With cool calmness. A brown stain frowned from her purple t-shirt. The calmness in her eyes trembled upon feeling the cold sand.

"I am me," I said. "I am me, myself, and I. Only me, not you, not anyone else."

Her head bowed in acceptance. But she didn't say anything.

"You shall apologize for your actions."

Her mouth opened, but I wouldn't let her speak, "You shall apologize and admit your fault. In front of everyone."

The brown eyes peeked at me questioningly. "In front of you?"

"In front of everyone, including me."

Warm wind came from the right and without any warning it blew onto the earth and up again, dragging the sand after it, creating a fog so thick that the silhouette of the other me was lost behind it. "All right," I heard her say before dust covered the words and the world faded before me.

When the mist finally melted, high walls of crimson seats arranged in a wide semicircle and slopes of golden ornaments surrounded me, the teeny-tiny creature that could be barely seen from up there. All the seats, all the balconies, even the stage and the orchestra pit, were crowded.

My own voice called from somewhere in the audience, "You shall apologize and admit your fault. In front of everyone. Including me."

"I am me!" I shouted, but no sound came out.

The high roof collapsed, the shining chandelier sank, with each of its thousand candles falling in a different direction, turning into colorful dust before they reached the floor, piling on the velvet-covered seats and adorning the heads of the viewers that crumbled into powder, too. Before me now was the transparent skyscraper, with all my colleagues and employees pressing onto the glass walls to catch a glimpse of me.

"I am myself!" I yelled.

With a terrible blow, the glass broke, shedding shards on the computers, wires, plants, people, the walls that also turned into shards leaking into the computers, wires, plants, people, and walls of the floor beneath, and so on, and so on, like a gigantic domino, until the building disappeared. Instead, the peeling brick block arose, whose windows were so small and dirty that I could not see the inside.

"I am I!" I cried.

One of the walls was aggressively smashed, as if a child dissatisfied with his creation kicked his building blocks castle, and the bricks hit the others and the ones near them. They fell to the ground like a pile of bones. Children's laughter followed the destruction and little fingers reached for the blocks that were now less than five centimeters wide. The chatter of older students and gossip of the others covered them from above; the noise of the entire school attacked me from all sides.

"It's me!" I screamed so wildly that my voice broke. Unable to breathe, I buried my face in my hands and realized it was wet with tears.

"It's me!" I panted again and again until suddenly I could hear my whisper. The noise disappeared.

I raised my head and found Myself at home. She was standing in the living room, barefoot, the high heels on the Persian carpet, in her sleek gold evening dress, the diamond necklace and earrings in her hand. Through the large windows I could see that the sky outside was pitch black. All the lights were turned on, but did not stop the night from seeping in. Me didn't move, only watched me with vague surprise.

It took me some time to realize that I was standing in the

same position, watching her.

"It's me," she said at last.

"It's me," I echoed.

"Which me?" she asked.

"The only me," I replied.

"How can you tell?"

The light caught my attention. Dark steam was coming out of it, curling and waving and gradually sinking to the parquet. I sighed with disappointment. I bought that light in Spain, cost more than my grand piano.

"How can *you* tell?" I tore my eyes from the ceiling and focused back on Me.

"Do you think you could?"

"Do you think *you* could?"

The smoke continued creeping down the walls, mixing with the night coming from the windows.

"Maybe I could."

"Maybe *I* could."

A dark pool accumulated on the floor, flowing around our ankles.

"Who? You or me?"

"Who are you?"

"Who is you?"

"Who is Me?"

"Who is I?"

The smoke stuck to the ceiling and to the windowsills. It rested on the gold dress, on the brown hair, on the diamond jewels. It dropped through the long eyelashes into the serious brown eyes.

I remained in complete darkness.

ALONE

He took out the white card, placed it on the box by the door and anxiously waited to hear the beep. It greeted him after a brief moment and unlocked the door. The noise of his steps was swallowed by a brown carpet stretched from wall to wall. The room was quite small. A narrow bed, a little table, an old-fashioned phone, and an empty flowerpot were the only pieces of furniture. There was also an immense mirror covering the entire opposite wall.

He rested his suitcase on the floor and landed on the bed with a sigh. This was certainly not the room he hoped for, but it was good enough for one night. He looked at the mirror and started unbuttoning his shirt, sweaty from travel. He jerked with alarm as his reflection moved. His reflection moved. And he didn't.

It got up from the bed, walking toward the mirror, where it stopped, throwing confused glances at the room.

The man observed, frozen with terror.

"Hello," said the reflection.

"Hello," he uttered.

"Will you be staying in this room?" the other one asked.

"Yes…" he replied.

"Well, I guess we'll be kind of sharing it. This wall is glass, you see," he knocked on the mirror, "so it's as if the rooms weren't divided at all."

An uncontrollable fit of laughter escaped him. "Oh, I thought it was a mirror! Boy, did you scare me!"

The other man laughed, too. "It is confusing, isn't it?"

"What kind of hotel doesn't divide the rooms?"

"A really bad one."

He laughed again. "Anyway, I'll be staying only for one night, so I hope I won't disturb you."

"Me too, so we're even," said the man with a smile, "I'm Charles, by the way."

"Really?" He was taken aback. "That's my name, too."

They engaged in a conversation. They seemed to have everything in common. Both headed to the capital for a meeting and they had practically the same job. Both had the same blond hair and blue suit. Also, they shared the same interests: both loved coffee and chess.

"My wife was furious when I told her I had to leave again," he mentioned.

"Mine too; she almost called my boss to complain."

"Women, huh?"

They chuckled.

"Excuse me, I'll just go to the bathroom," said Charles and left.

Upon finding himself alone, he raised the phone receiver, dialing to reception. A pleasant voice of a woman answered him.

"Hello, I call from room 101. I thought I'd be alone."

"You are alone," said the voice.

"I'm sorry, I don't think you understand. I seem to be sharing the room with someone else, but I was originally told that I'd be spending a night in a single room."

"You are."

"But it's connected to the adjacent room. There's another person with me."

"You are alone."

Outraged, Charles slammed the phone down. "Can't even make a complaint anymore," he murmured. He didn't last long in this state of mind, as his companion quickly returned.

"So tell me something about your family," Charles encouraged him to talk.

"Well, I have three beautiful kids; my oldest daughter just started high school."

"She did, didn't she?"

They continued talking, racing to tell as much information as possible before the other had a chance to do so. Their past was alike, their present seemed the same, and they were perfect reflections of each other; yet neither of them seemed to accept the fact.

"My mother died last year."

"Because of cancer."

"The kids miss her a great deal."

"Of course they do."

They talked on, refusing to lose the informal competition. Smile after smile, word after word, phrase after phrase.

"I'm planning a trip to Germany."

"To visit an old friend."

"We haven't seen each other in twenty years."

Phrase after phrase, word after word, smile after smile.

"I just finished reading *Lord of the Flies*."

"Wanted to know what they make my son read."

"I didn't like it at all."

"Couldn't see the point."

The conversation went on. Both headed to the capital for a meeting and they had practically the same job. Both had the same blond hair and blue suit. Also, they shared the same interests: both loved coffee and chess.

And they talked.

*****

The clock struck half past eleven. Harriet Parks, dressed in her white housekeeping uniform, locked the door of the room she had just exited and pushed her cart forward. She left it in front of room 101. The room was a perfect copy of all the others; it had the same carpet, bed, table, phone, and flowerpot. The only difference between them was the mirror on the wall. Upon entering, she saw a man lying on the floor, his fingers pressed against the cracked mirror in a restless, frozen twitch. The carpet was colored with his dry blood.

The man was apparently by himself when it happened.

And yet there were too many people.

DEAR WIND

She walked into the hall, looking around for the ticket stand. Small groups of people stood here and there, chatting, but she didn't notice them, staring at the decorative ceiling. The copula was illustrated with dozens of figures, drawn carefully with faint colors, fading into each other, yet remaining separate. They turned and swung motionlessly, their reds and blues and yellows, all watery, immersed with countless dots of paint. Everything, creatures and objects alike, blended into a colorful turbulence trapped inside a baroque chapel, roaring and besieging the copula in a desperate attempt to escape into the vast sky.

With difficulty, she lowered her gaze and waited for the storm to dissipate. As soon as all its remains sank and covered her memories in a thin layer of colorful dust, she looked around the hall again. The ticket stand was merely a chair surrounded by a wall of banana boxes. She crossed the marble floor and stopped in front of it. A pair of bright blue eyes smiled at her from behind the improvised counter.

"Would you like to buy tickets for the ceramics class?"

She stared at the girl behind the banana boxes for a while, diving unwittingly into her own thoughts. The girl was about her age, perhaps a little older. Her round cheeks were flushed, her smile small and delicate. Her light hair, too, was fine and thin, glistening under the light of the large lamps above. Her entire figure was that of a beautiful porcelain doll, defenseless against the wind.

"Would you like to buy tickets for the ceramics class?" the girl asked again, smiling.

Embarrassment seized her, as it did so often, and she looked at the thin fingers that rested on the banana carton to avoid the smile in her eyes. She was standing in front of a woman her age, asking for a childish ceramics class. Why did she decide to come in the first place? The idea of leaving seduced her for a second, but then she remembered the reason for her visit.

She nodded.

"Great. How many?"

The girl probably thought she was there with her family. Or with a small child.

"Two," she murmured, sticking to the idea.

"What's your name?" asked the porcelain maiden as she scribbled numbers and letters on the paper straps.

"What is *your* name?" she answered after wincing with a start.

The girl looked up. A hint of confusion mirrored in her eyes, but quickly disappeared behind the welcoming smile. "Helen."

"You're surrounded by banana boxes, Helen," she said.

"Yes, I know." Helen laughed, but insisted on her question. "I have to write your name on the tickets."

"Iphigenia," she said reluctantly.

Helen wrote it down on both papers, without asking whether she had spelled it correctly. Then she handed them to Iphigenia in exchange for a few coins, which she hid in one of the boxes.

"Here you go. The entrance is on the left."

Iphigenia folded the tickets and buried them in her pocket. She walked to the center of the room, even though she knew that she could be easily distinguished from the crowd. Girls like Helen always perturbed her a little. Girls that were prettier than her, shorter than her, nicer than her. She didn't envy them, they just made her think less of herself.

Iphigenia reached into her pocket again and took the tickets out. She feared they might fall out and preferred to hold them in her hands. *Why would I buy an extra ticket?* she asked herself, searching for a plausible excuse that could have possibly provided an explanation for Helen and the other people that might notice her.

She was probably taking a little child for a fun afternoon. But what child? Her child? What eighteen-year-old has a child? That didn't make sense. A younger sibling? She was too old for that. A cousin. Iphigenia smiled. She was taking care of her five-year-old cousin while his parents were out of town. That could occur to anyone.

Now she wanted to get rid of the extra ticket. She decided to give it to someone, to give some child a fun afternoon after all. Still deep in thought, she made her way back to the main door and pushed the ticket into the hand of the first person who came in. Without bothering to look at his face, she turned around and went to stand in the line for the ceramics class.

There were many families, just as she had expected, with little kids running around or sleeping in their strollers, either screaming, laughing, complaining, or crying. She found it strange that people considered pottery childish. What child would ever be able to make a decent cup? They just get dirty and create a terrible mess. But still…there was something about pottery that drew her to it as a child. It was the attempt to recreate the childhood of her dreams that brought her into this place.

"Childhood is the basis of a person's life. Without a past — there is no future," said Kate when Iphigenia had brought the subject up.

A little girl bumped into her train of thought. For a moment their eyes met, then the child ran back to her parents, sank into her stroller and fastened herself, forgetting Iphigenia's existence altogether.

Iphigenia followed her with her eyes. She observed her clumsy moves, her hurried steps, her chubby limbs moving along with her yet shapeless hips. The child had dark hair, significantly shortened by ringlet curls, and brown eyes, wide open with invisible eyelashes. Another child, somewhat older, ran toward the stroller with two stuffed penguins under her arm.

"Why did you throw him, Nelly? He's hurting!" said the child to the one in the stroller, "Look, he's bleeding!"

Nelly only turned the other way.

"Nelly, give him a plaster." And the penguin landed on Nelly's lap.

"I want the other one," whined Nelly as she tried to push the toy aside.

"No, you hurt this one. See?" she pointed, sticking her finger deep into the fabric. "Give him a plaster."

Apparently, Nelly didn't care about the injured penguin. She turned around, sitting up as high as possible and reached out to touch her mother's hand, which rested on the stroller's back. "Mommy, I want that thing!"

She had to repeat the declaration numerous times to get her mother's attention.

"What thing?"

A plump finger pointed at a tiny bottle of hand gel tied to the stroller.

"That's for cleaning our hands later," answered mommy, who continued conversing with her husband.

"I want it now!" exclaimed Nelly.

"What about the penguin?"

Iphigenia forced herself to focus on her own feet. Watching the family so closely had made her uncomfortable. She felt that she entered a kind of bubble that divided them from the rest of the world, a bubble whose purpose was to keep away strangers like herself. In spite of that, she suddenly felt close to the little girl in the stroller. She felt as if they were somehow alike, maybe even the same. Their appearance was different, their manner, lifestyle, and family, but they both had a thing in common. Iphigenia knew that they were both lost. At last she couldn't control herself any longer and glanced at the stroller again to see the two girls rubbing and smelling their hands contentedly.

At that moment, the line moved again, and eight people disappeared behind the wooden doors. Those doors disturbed Iphigenia. They were like a patch on an expensive evening dress; they ruined the hall's harmony, destroyed its beauty, barricaded the flow of the colors on the walls.

Iphigenia shook her head violently, raising the color-dust to cover this newest memory, spraying dead art on a modern door. She preferred the dead art. She liked the dead art.
A dim voice was heard behind this temporary curtain in her mind. She thought it called her name. She shook her head again.

"You're just being paranoid," she said, repeating Kate's words.

The line moved again, and this time she passed through the wooden door.

The spacey room was that of a barn, and a smell of wood chips and hay filled the still air. Eight old-fashioned pottery wheels, each with a large box of clay next to it, stood in two lines, divided by big gaps.

The peace was immediately disturbed by the visitors' voices.

"Grab a seat!" said a woman's voice somewhere in the room.

Without waiting for further instructions, Iphigenia sank to the chair by the closest wheel, upon which there still lay a handful of shapeless clay. She automatically dipped her hands in a bowl full of water, gently touched the clay from both sides, and started spinning.

A sudden memory arose from the storm in her mind, floating on the crying wind far above the others, clear and bright. An elderly man sitting by a wooden pottery wheel, his back bent beneath an invisible burden, his hands gray with dry clay, spinning, spinning. He struck fear into Iphigenia when she was but seven years old, but then, only after his death, she started liking the old neighbor and his mysterious art. Iphigenia often related to people after their death. She liked many dead people.

They all went through the unavoidable, through what she was too afraid to understand. In her mind, they were heroes, but she knew every living creature sooner or later takes the same, brave last step.

"You're doing this all wrong," she suddenly heard the woman's voice above her head. Two strong hands stuck to hers and guided their movements for a long while. Then the hands disappeared.

Iphigenia felt a familiar pain in her chest, as if she swallowed a big chunk of food that burned her from the inside on its way to her stomach. She could only stare at her dry fingers as it made its way slowly to the top of the pain-hill inside her. It had started a few years ago, and grew rapidly worse. The slightest comment sent such a signal through her, not different from those she felt during the most difficult moments of her life. She never told anyone, and only waited for each impulse to pass, because it was only a creation of her fantasy. Lately, however, she could feel them piling up inside, sticking to each other, melting into each other, burning her with desperation. She was suffocating.

What is it like, Iphigenia thought, *to be dead? To be gone? To become a part of the land all my successors will step on?* When the glitter in the eyes, the color in the cheeks, the wind in the head turn gray, as did her fingers this very moment, while touching a tiny bit of clay. Sometimes she wished to go through this now, without delay, to end all the fear and uncertainty, but she never did. What would her mother say if she did?

The clay accumulated beneath her fingernails, dry and itchy, but she liked it, feeling full of something that was not a part of her or a part of her thoughts. Or a part of Kate's thoughts.
"I'm here for you. Always," she said. Iphigenia was grateful for that, but sometimes even Kate's caring advice suffocated her.

The endless spinning move stopped when her hand trembled involuntarily. She heard someone calling her name again. And again. Every time it came a little closer. She bit her lips until a metallic taste of blood filled her mouth. She bent closer to the gray mass spinning round and round, wishing to get sucked into it, to merge into this eternal, calm movement.

She regretted the idea as soon as it crossed her mind, cursing herself. *What would mother say?*

"Iphigenia?" This time her name was too close to ignore. She looked up.

The voice belonged to a tall lad with black, short hair and a polo t-shirt. He stared at her with a mixture of curiosity and eagerness.

"Are you Iphigenia?" he repeated.

She nodded and focused on the wheel again, hoping he'd go away.

"You gave me your ticket."

She didn't answer.

"But you're here so…I guess you had an extra one."

Iphigenia sighed.

"I'd like to thank you."

She looked straight into his brown eyes. "You're welcome." *There. Now he'll leave.*

But instead he sat, smiling, on the floor next to her, revealing a line of perfect teeth. "I took my little cousin out for a fun afternoon; his parents are out of town." He laughed, "Look, I'm sorry to interrupt, but when I saw the name on the ticket, I just had to meet you, you see. " After a moment he added, "It's an amazing coincidence."

When Iphigenia didn't answer, he winked, as if he just remembered something, and quickly explained. "I'm Llesy!"

The burning feeling attacked her again. She needed to be alone. "OK," she told him.

"That's a pet name for Achilles."

"Oh."

"No, you probably don't understand, in the Greek

mythology, Iphigenia was supposed to…"

"Yes, I know," she stopped him, "shouldn't you be with your cousin?"

"The instructor is taking care of him. I can stay for a while. Who are you with?"

Iphigenia gave up and turned toward him, leaning on her thighs, her dirty palms hanging between her legs. "With Kate." It wasn't a lie. Kate was always with her, inside her mind.

"Who's Kate?"

"A friend." *My only friend.*

The following moment of silence was interrupted by his hearty laugh. "My mom named me. She always has such crazy ideas. But my brother's name is Rick, so…" he shrugged and laughed again. "What about you?"

"Mom's idea."

"Crazy, huh?"

A violent gust of wind blew inside her, raising the calm dust, moving the organized thoughts into chaos. It burned her eyes and found its way out through her words. "She happens to be brilliant," she exclaimed, "she finished high school by the time she was sixteen and runs four companies. She loves me with all her heart and she'd die if something happened to me."

Llesy moved a little further, shocked. "Sorry, I was just joking," he mumbled, "why should something happen to you?"

Iphigenia bit her lips again. She couldn't answer. She had been asking herself the same question over and over, but couldn't find an answer.

She captured his eyes one more time, knowing he'd understand. For some reason she suddenly wanted him to understand.

A troubled wrinkle appeared on Llesy's forehead. He looked at her for a long time, trying to find a clue in her eyes. He understood.

"I'm sorry you have to deal with this. I shouldn't have told you."

"No, it's OK," he smiled, but his lower lip trembled, "I'm glad you did."

The class ended and Iphigenia got up, but Llesy followed her back to the hall.

"Are you a student?" He waited, and then added, "Do you work?"

She shook her head. "I'm taking a break."

Llesy smiled. "From what?"

"Everything. To organize my thoughts. Kate's idea."

"Oh yeah, you said she was here with you. Shouldn't we wait for her?"

"Shouldn't you wait for your cousin?" she hissed, crossing

her arms on her chest. Gray stains appeared on her blouse.

"Seriously, where is Kate?"

"At home," said Iphigenia reluctantly.

"Then why did you say she was here?"

"Because it was her idea."

"The break?"

She turned around and walked away, Llesy running after her.

"You talk too much," Iphigenia whispered.

"I'm curious!"

"Don't follow me just because you think you have to. You don't." With these words they entered the locker room where Iphigenia had left her bag earlier. The metal box trembled when she pressed the key into the hole. The lockers shivered down the row, pushing the signal from box to box, from wall to wall. The rows beneath and above soaked it gradually until only a slight trickle remained. Then they were tranquil, removing the signal from its point of origin by widening circles, like a lake swallowing the memory of a cast stone.

Iphigenia nodded. This was what she had to achieve; to forget, to tame the wild winds inside her, to accept everything and everyone into her own general silence.

"Relax! It isn't that hard when you get used to it," she mumbled one of Kate's favorite exclamations.

Carefully, so she didn't disturb the slumbering room, she picked up her bag. A mirror caught her attention on the way to the door, or rather the reflection in the mirror. Her clothes were spotted with mud, her fingers looked modeled from ash, dark circles lay beneath her narrowed eyes. Llesy's reflection behind her stood straight and lively. Only a few shallow wrinkles between his eyebrows remained from their previous conversation.

"I have to change."

It took him a moment to understand. His smile disappeared suddenly, but hurried to reappear. "I'll meet you outside." Then he left.

There was no bathroom, but she found a sink next to the door. The clear water passed through her fingers and became contaminated. Once clean, Iphigenia rubbed her hands on her jeans and stood in front of the mirror again. She remembered packing extra clothes the night before, just in case something happened. The idea occurred to her when she was laying in bed, waiting for the night's stillness to overcome the tired breeze blowing through her mind. It forced her to get up into the cold of the room and grope around in search for the wardrobe.

She gazed with surprise at the dress that awaited her inside the bag. This couldn't be called an extra piece of clothing just in case.

Iphigenia changed anyway. She regretted it as soon as she saw herself in the mirror, but couldn't change back to the wet, dirty clothes that lay on the floor by her feet. Not only was the dress impudently pink, it was also long; the skirt slid to the ground, covering her feet. Neat, almost invisible folds highlighted her exposed shoulders and the loose sleeves tickled her arms as she moved. She felt ridiculous.

Llesy, however, didn't seem to mind the dress. A wide smile spread over his face when she exited. "My fairy queen," he said as he walked by her side toward the large wooden door, toward the blue sky behind it. Iphigenia blushed.

A whistle pierced her thought, a sudden cry. The wind was rebelling, the wind was reminding her of its presence. It picked up her torn memories, carrying them to and fro; Kate, her mother, the curly-haired child with the stuffed penguin, Llesy's unexpected appearance. The wind split into countless flowing currents, whistling, revolting. Only now, at this uprise did she realize what she had done. She told Llesy about her wind. Nobody knew about her wind before. She shivered.

It was too late. Llesy recognized it. His hard, warm fingers touched hers for a brief moment, trying to get her attention. He drove the storm away like a blazing summer sun. "That's my cousin," he pointed at a little boy, about seven years old, standing near the barn door. He waved at him. "I have to take him home. Do you mind if we don't take the bus? It's really close."

Meanwhile, the little boy ran toward them, his steps echoing from the floor to the ceiling. "Who is she?" he asked, pointing at her with his tanned hand.

"This is Iphigenia," answered Llesy and grabbed the child's pointing hand.

"Another girl?" This comment made Llesy look away with embarrassment. "What about Diana?"

"We're taking a break." This time he wasn't talking to his cousin.

The three of them left the chapel and followed the gravel road outside. It crawled before them, revealing a little part of it at a time, letting them diverge from puddles or lose its track amongst the bushes and roots. The path went on, trusting them to follow it, through the gardens, through the graveyard. Iphigenia focused on her feet, careful not to glance at the black stones surrounding them. She let herself follow Llesy's wide strides, relieved.

Soon, they reached the streets behind the barred monastery gates and stopped by a yellow house with a red roof. The little boy unlocked the door, waved at Llesy, and disappeared inside.

"So your mother owns companies?" asked Llesy as they continued following the sidewalk.

Iphigenia nodded.

"What about your father?"

"Forestry."

He glanced at her. "Really? Wow! Does he hunt?"

"Deer."

"That's incredible. You know, Diana does this campaign about protecting wildlife."

She didn't really listen, but she let him talk. She noticed they were getting farther and farther from the streets and from the houses, and that the young trees at the edge of the forest surrounded them. A light breeze caressed Iphigenia's hair. It melted into her own wind, flowing in and out through her, rubbing gently against her forgotten dreams. It wished to console her, to show her that telling Llesy was unnecessary. The wind gathered fallen leaves from the mossy ground and danced with them until they were embraced by the horizon; it whistled through the cones in the far tree tops, jingled the sleepy acorns. She remembered the winter when she left seeds on her windowsill and songbirds came, grateful to eat. She remembered her first trip to this forest, how she had found a spring colder than early morning. She remembered finding an injured rabbit that did not fear her and let her help him. She remembered Kate's last argument: "but you have so many nice memories, your life is beautiful," and she knew it was true. She had never forgotten that. But this only made her feel worse.

Ungrateful, selfish, foolish. She chastised herself. Another heavy, hot impulse sank inside her. Iphigenia stopped walking, her eyes fixed on the pink skirt that looked even frillier on the dark forest ground. She shook her head.

Once again she felt Llesy's strong fingers touching her arm, for less than a second, then they left. She looked up. He did not look at her; he was looking at a deer about ten meters away.

The delicate animal was lying on its side, its slender legs spread helplessly and its graceful neck stretched, as if it were reaching out for something. It was dead.

The sound of snapping twigs indicated someone was coming from the other side of the forest, and a few moments later Iphigenia's father, dressed in his leather jacket, emerged from the bushes. He smiled and knelt by the deer.

Llesy's wrinkles reappeared. "What will Diana say?"

The wind attacked her in a loud thunderstorm, shouting, crying, snatching words, beating thoughts, mixing her entire being. She started running, trying to outrun it, to leave it behind. She reached the cliffs, hoping the storm would escape from her mind into that large space, fill the crack between the sky and the chasm. But it wouldn't let go, it pushed her identity aside, swirled all the memories into a loud tornado. Her past, her future, her mother, her father, Kate, Llesy, the lost child in the stroller, they all became a dusty cloud of ache inside her head. She breathed heavily, waving her arms and pulling her hair, desperately seeking a way, a path through which she could drive the pain away. The wind turned, the wind whistled, the wind raged.

Then there was silence.

The wind was replaced by calmness, by nothingness. At that moment Iphigenia knew that she was alone. Without Llesy, without Kate, without the everlasting breeze. She'd do anything to escape the stillness, to hear the wind again.

Her hair flew around her face and into her eyes as the wind came back, just before she hit the ground.

BLOOD RELATION

The crows flew above the valley, their ebony wings sliding upon the whistles of the wind, their cawing merging with its sudden cries. The currents chased each other restlessly, zigzagging and turning, light bouncing off their invisible scales, their transparent teeth shining amidst their withdrawn lips, ready to bite the head of their enemy or their own curved tale that got in their way. They all ran and flew and turned and turned, and sank lower and lower, until the last stable of grass bowed before their blind power, but ascended just before touching the cold ground, the dirt. Wild as they were, beautiful as they were, invisible as they were, they could not touch the dirt. Upwards the currents rose, to where the dust and grass stables could not get, and could only look upwards, searching for the unseen glorious creatures, for the legendary wind, waiting to be caressed.

The crowds were standing motionless, each on either hill, facing each other without perceiving. Their armor glittered in the sun, and their pale faces peeking from the graceless helmets were bathed in the beams. An occasional jingle crossed the dense air in the shallow chasm, followed by the muffled sound of heavy movements. Each member of each crowd, each pawn, each knight, each king, was clad from head to toe in heavy sheets of iron, fishing nets of tinkling rings, thick woolen sleeves, thin leather caps, running streams of sweat. The revealed faces only gazed at the rivals on the opposite hill, one with a wandering stare, one biting their lips, one frowning, one panting; all serious, all waiting.

Let us take a step back and see the bigger picture. Two groups of men on two green hills beneath the sunny sky and weight of tons of metal with the blowing wind and valley between them. What were the winds and valley? What barrier did these few kilometers make? And yet the border was clear. This is one side, that is the other. This is my side, that is yours.

A shriek of a blowing horn pierced the air in the valley and shooed away the crows. Like piles of bugs spilling out of buckets, the crowds rolled down the hills, hurtled into the valley, and became one swarm, moving chaotically and buzzing a mixture of shouts, stomps, gasps, and clacks. Above the field fly the crows, circling slowly, their ebony wings sliding upon the whistles of the wind, their cawing merging with its sudden cries, watching the shiny insects, waiting for their feast.

***

Skolla waded through the valley. She could feel the warm sun touching her back, grasping her hair with its prolonging fingers, desperately trying not to sink into the horizon. The summer winds swiftly crept toward it as it inhaled its last breath, and, for a moment, Skolla was walking against a low, warm current that ringed her ankles as it passed by. An urge to look down entered her. She suppressed it. Blood didn't normally bother her, but after a fight she couldn't stand it. Especially after a few hours, at dawn, when flies and mosquitoes defiled the lifeless brownish heaps scattered all around.

Her boots clicked on the stone floor as she finally entered the bathroom. The blurry hill could be seen through the frosted glass, the valley full of all the debris clearly at the entrance, in the place of the missing wall. The ceiling was also partly missing; it covered the shower, which was also protected by another layer of closer frosted glass walls and a piece of the sink. Barely noticing the copying moves of the woman in the mirror, she stooped and started unlatching her light armor. Most of it was stained by dry mud, grass, leaves, sweat, bird droppings, and what seemed to be more dry mud. Here and there, however, a shiny bit of steel shone from between the filthy rest. Like her right breast. The boys must have noticed that. She couldn't help smiling. After getting rid of the burdensome shell, Skolla turned to the mirror, stepping on the chest piece on the floor. She tore a square of toilet paper, opened the faucet to make sure the water was cold, wetted the paper carefully, and leaned closer before raising it toward her face. She examined the countless scarlet specks that stuck to her cheek and forehead with her usual lack of interest. They reminded her a little of ripe pomegranate seeds, little smelly rubies that dimly reflected the light cast on them by the lamp above her head. The red bumps melted immediately under the toilet paper's wet swipes. She paused for a while after coloring the square. Half her cheek was dotted, the other snow-white. *Which is better,* she asked herself, *living flesh that tasted the blood of others or one that did the same but denies it?*

"Hey!"

Skolla's hand jumped to the hilt. Her grip tightened as she spun toward the missing wall.

The voice belonged to Hatti. Skolla knew that very well before her harsh tone sank to a soft approximant sound.

She was dressed in a cloak, her braided hair hidden beneath the hood, leather arm protectors stretching from her fingers to the elbows. The darkness was now so thick that she was barely visible. Only the star at the top of her pointed dagger shone from the night.

"What?" Skolla spat.

Hatti didn't move, as if hesitating, but then she took a few quick steps, moving sideways and a little forward but not entering the lit bathroom.

"Is that mum's perfume?" she asked at last, questioningly, her dagger still ready for attack.

"Yeah, so?" Skolla replied, "Mum wanted me to have it."

A worried thought passed Hatti's face, the dagger lowered a little. "Are you using it right now? You should save it…"

"No, I'm not. I was just washing my face, if you must know. What are you doing here?"

The dagger rose to its previous position. "I am armed."

"So am I. What are you doing here?"

Hatti's shoulders rose and sank again beneath the heavy cloak. "Nothing."

"Nothing? So I suppose you would sneak into the enemy's camp and risk your head just like that? You are here because they offered you candy if you crept over here and nosed around."

"No!"

"Really? So you changed your mind and acknowledged your fault? Realized that you joined a bunch of brutes? That is not as likely."

"No!" Her voice was trembling. Whether with anger or humiliation Skolla couldn't tell. "I came because of you."

"You came to me? Did you trip and fall and you need a kiss? Oh, come to your sister!" She spread her arms in a mockingly welcoming gesture, the sword still in her right hand. Hatti took a few steps back.

Skolla smiled, turning back to the mirror and tearing a new square of toilet paper. "Get lost before I have to kill you."

"I need information."

"Mmmmhmmm," the long shadows of her brow and nose hindered as she tried to wipe away the pomegranate seeds.

"I need to know what happened that night."

The paper sank slowly, swinging from side to side, white against the dark surroundings, like a lost feather falling from the night sky. She turned around slowly, her loose hair falling to her back, her lips pressed, her eyes fixed on the cloak-wrapped figure standing in front of her but at the same time staring into an empty, infinite space. The sword hit the bathroom floor with a loud clash. She didn't need it. She didn't want it. It was…alien. It fell on the pile of dirty metal pieces, of empty metal pieces.

"That night…

***

I was taking the bus to that school dad wanted see. I didn't really want to go; I didn't believe I would get in anyway. Still, he wanted to go there, he said he'll meet me at the bus stop at eight. The vehicle was crammed. Luckily, I took a seat by the window so I was farther from the crowded aisle and a little more comfortable. I got much less comfortable when a group of old ladies entered and had nowhere to sit. I would have gotten up but the person on the seat next to me wouldn't move. I watched their thin shaky legs nervously, holding my breath every time the bus wobbled. At last the person next to me got up. By then I noticed that even though there were more and more empty seats, the old women remained standing. Gradually, the bus became less crowded, people getting off outnumbered those getting on; they switched and switched until the vehicle was almost empty. I watched them passing through the squeaky, greasy doors, leaving the illuminated gas-scented aisle and fading into the unknown. Every time the doors opened, the outside seemed darker. By the time I got off, I knew, the sky would be completely black. I would probably mingle with it; disappear amongst the darkness-covered world. I could picture it, a long silk sheet of night protecting frames of mantelpieces and round tables from the accumulating dust.

I was wearing black jeans, my favorite black shirt, and a black headband with a bow held my hair back. I nodded to myself. I would definitely disappear.

Passengers kept switching, three got off, two got on, two got off, one got on. Except for the driver's vague silhouette in the front, I was alone. There were no more hurrying people to observe and the doors remained shut; soon I felt my own stare crawling up my back. It must have been mine; I was alone, except for the driver's vague silhouette in the front.

My patience was slowly leaving me, staying behind mixed with the gas cloud defecated by the bus. The previous stop seemed too long ago. I looked out the windows but found no clue to where I was as they were stuffed by the darkness. I looked at my watch but could not read it as I couldn't distinguish the hands from the shadows. At last my thoughts, like my patience, escaped the rusty tin walls surrounding me and travelled home, to the little wooden steps, through the beaded curtain, to the little bedroom, to the veranda. They ran around the house, checking that everything was in place, including little Hatti, just like it was when I left. I could almost feel the warm floor beneath my feet, smell the white rice in the bowls on the table.

And I regretted I didn't stay. I wished I never got on that bus. I knew that everything had changed since I left a few hours ago. The rice was surely eaten, the floor was probably covered with crumbles, Hatti could have gone to bed. And I was stuck, in a rickety bus going from nowhere to nowhere, leaving everything behind, frozen in the past for what at the moment seemed like eternity. Later I would find out that it *did* freeze in my past for eternity.

Suddenly the doors opened with a loud wail, and before I even realized what I was doing, I jumped through them. A few blinks afterwards I found myself standing at the bus stop beneath a street light. A few people stood nearby, the road was calm, only the far off sound of wind sliding off car windshields was heard in the distance. There was no trace of the bus.

The fresh air brushed away the aching thoughts and I sneered at my doubts. Everything was going to be fine. I was going to be fine.

I can't really remember what happened then, how long I was walking or which streets I passed. I remember the school door. It was tall, immensely tall and narrow, its top was hidden somewhere in the sky. It looked like a vertical crevasse, cold yet overly inviting. The doors inside were very similar, only a little wider, the roof was seemingly missing. The only differences between the outside and inside were the groups of people here and there, the lanced window frames on the walls, and stone statues lying on the ground. For some reason I felt detached. Everything around me was misty, unreal.

"What are those statues?" I uttered to myself after a while.

I didn't need an answer. I realized they were tombstones.

I approached one, out of curiosity, even though it was too dark to read the carved letters. The rough features of the stone knight lying on the tomb could be distinguished, though. His gray hair lay loosely around his gray head and on his gray brow, his gray eyes wide open, his gray tense arteries visible on his gray neck, his gray fingers resting on his long sword that was not gray, but had a reddish hint beneath a layer of turquoise.

With some difficulty, I tore my stare from the sleeping statue and crossed the room, entering another one to see a forming line. Without thinking twice, I joined the line, as did others behind me.

"Why are we waiting in line?" I asked after a while and turned around, hoping those behind me might know.

My eyes met the gaze of two ice-colored balls. They belonged to a thin, no, skinny man towering above all the others. I could not determine whether his lips were drawn back in a smile or threat. He reminded me of the stone knight, even though they were ridiculously different. I also knew that he wasn't really there, perhaps he was the embodiment of my imagination, but somehow he seemed more real than everything else. Somehow, he pierced the barrier between me and the rest of the world. Somehow, that moment changed my life. For eternity.

I didn't take the bus back. I relied on my own legs to carry me home.

***

Hatti's hood fell back as she shook her head. "You're just saying that. You modify the past to fit what you know

now."

"No, I don't," Skolla leaned on the sink, "now get lost."

Hatti didn't move.

"What else do you want?"

"To hear what really happened. The whole story."

"I have already told you."

Hatti crossed her arms on her chest. She stepped forward, but didn't enter the bathroom. She remained there, a figure on the border between light and dark.

"What really happened?" she asked.

"Ok, what really happened?" echoed Skolla.

Hatti's hands fell to her sides, dangling lifelessly. "That night…

***

I was home alone. Skolla had left a few hours earlier. She ate dinner at five; I was just watching her take the rice, spoon by spoon, out of her bowl. My toys, too, were sitting on the wooden floor in a long line facing her and watching. Some of them hesitated a few times and cast a questioning glance at me. *Why are we watching Skolla eat?* I shrugged. Only the frog wouldn't take its eyes off her. It was hungry.

For me, five was too soon for dinner. If I ate at five, I'd have to go to sleep earlier. I didn't want that. Also, the day was not even near the end, but I had to admit it was getting quite dark outside.

Skolla was applying her well known practice of ignoring us.

To any other person she would have seemed calm, but I recognized her quick glances to the low right corner of the room and the quick, quiet chewing and knew that she wasn't that easy after all. When she got up and opened the door, she left her bowl on the table.

We remained seated, me and my stuffed animals, in line on the floor. When five long minutes passed and there was no sign of Skolla coming back, I lept to her seat, crossed my legs, and touched the very tip of the spoon while assuming her position. Frog could smell the little rice left in the bowl and looked at me with a mixture of anger and pleading. I smiled and threw a grain into Frog's interdigital webbing. Then I gasped and took the grain back before Frog could eat it and put it back in the bowl. *I moved the rice. I'm sitting in Skolla's place. Something's changed. Something's wrong.* I tried to picture the scene from a different angle: the table, the bowls, the seated girl, and the line of toys on the floor. The change couldn't be that visible. From a long distance, I could be mistaken for Skolla, even though I was much shorter.

Carefully, I slid back to the floor and joined my toys. They weren't surprised and after a while we continued playing. That afternoon we had a tea party. Now that dad and Skolla weren't home, we could talk loudly and sing as much as we wanted. Yet it wasn't as fun as earlier, when Skolla was watching us quietly from her favorite seat. My animals grew more and more tired until they stopped talking altogether. I tried to wake them up, but their plush mouths wouldn't open and bead eyes wouldn't blink.

I stood up and made my way through the lifeless heaps toward the bedroom. A beaded curtain divided it from the living room and from the little steps leading in from the entrance. I felt warm currents of the home's smell encircling my ankles on their way down the stairs into the darkness, although they may have only been a fruit of my imagination.

I entered the bedroom and sank onto the bed. Not on my bed, but on the left side of dad's bed. Mum's bed. It had long stopped smelling like her, and that night it had no smell at all. Probably because all the smells had already left the house while I was entering the bedroom.

Lying on my back, I watched the strings of night sneaking in through the large window, flying through the air and weaving into a long silk sheet of night protecting frames of mantelpieces and round tables from the accumulating dust. In a few moments, I thought, it would hang on all the walls, swaying gently with the wind from outside. I would probably mingle with it; disappear amongst the darkness-covered room.

It was then, in the middle of this lonely darkness, that he came.

The steps were the first thing I noticed.

Then the slight creak as he stopped and remained motionless.

Then his soft breathing, in and out, in and out.

For hours, I listened to his wet breath, to the air clashing against his strong jaws. I listened to the crickets bathing in the moisture of the summer air. I listened to the blinking neighborhood in the distance, whose lit windows warmly assured me that we were alone.

"Ah," I let out a soft sigh. I had nothing to say but someone had to speak first.

Like dry shells on the sand grains by an ancient sea the

beads rustled behind my head. The wind caressed them gently so I knew that the window was open.

Then his voice entered, too, deep and dark, like a long lost legend of forests and meadows brought to the sea shells by the well-travelled breeze. "I am the wolf."

I knew that. I was told of the wolves many a time in the past. "I know," I replied.

"Do you know why I came?" His question leaped from among the crickets, seceded on the background of the night.

"You came because of me," I said.

"I came thanks to you."

I could picture his ears flattening onto his prolonged skull, ready to catch my answer before it could leave the room.

"Why are you a wolf?"

"Because I chose to be a wolf. It's not that hard."

I rested my head on my hand. "Can I be a wolf?"

"Everyone can be a wolf."

"Can Skolla become a wolf?"

"Everyone can be a wolf."

For a moment the sounds of the night were heard again.

"What would we do if we became wolves?" I asked at last.

"You'll chase each other."

"Will it be fun?"

"I don't know," he said.

"How come? You're a wolf."

"Yes, but not everyone is."

My eyes narrowed and suddenly I distinguished his two blue dog eyes from the darkness. My words melted into the air, "So there's no one to chase you…"

A spark appeared in the blue dog eyes. "You can chase me if you want."

I sat up in the bed, smiling, clapping my hands in playful joy. But then I shook my head. "If I was a wolf," I said, "I'd chase Skolla."

He didn't question my decision. Neither did I. That's what sisters do, is it not? They chase each other for ever and ever because it's so fun, it's so enraging, it's so unstoppable. That's what sisters do.

As I was pondering quietly, I heard him sniff. He was hungry. Barefooted, I stood up, passed the curtain with the sound of gentle rustle, and came to the plush stumps still scattered around the floor.

"You can have Frog," I said, picking it up, "he's hungry too."

For the rest of the night we just howled.

***

Now it was Skolla's turn to shake her head. "You were nine. You couldn't have remembered such a thing. Even if you were older, it was too long ago."

"It was ages ago, and still I remember."

Skolla sneered, "Oh really? We have fought and fought against everyone and everything, including time itself, until we got back to before the Stone Age, and then back to 2000 and something, and then back to the Stone Age and then back to 2000 and something more, and again and again because history is too short to provide enough space for such a fight, and you claim you still remember that night? Your story was absurd enough to prove you don't."

"Yeah, right, great point. Yours was way more absurd!" Her hand trembling with suppressed anger, Hatti dropped her dagger. A white scar pierced the stone floor.

"Well, cling to your little story while you still can."

"What's that supposed to mean?" Hatti shouted.

"We're trapped in this fight anyway, and one day or another you will forget the night that started it."

"And then?"

"Nothing. Then we will truly become wolves chasing each other from eternity to eternity, merciless beasts without a past or future. Wolves that hunt every living thing they encounter for no reason."

Hatti's lips curled in an animalistic hiss. "No! Don't say that! Besides, it's all your fault!"

Skolla exhaled loudly and hit the sink with her sword as she put it down. "My fault?"

"You're the one that left me alone that night!"

"You're the one that talked to the wolf!"

"You're the one that left home for some school!"

"You're the one that decided to join the wolves!"

"You're the one that deserted me, left me behind!"

"You're the one that became all violent for attention!"

"You're the one that stopped noticing me!"

"You didn't even understand what was going on!"

"You never bothered to explain!"

"You didn't know the difference! You don't remember her, do you?"

"So I don't remember mum as well as you, so what?"

"So, you stopped being my sister."

"Why?"

"Mum was the reason we were sisters."

"What about dad?"

"You claim he was a wolf, I claim he was a knight. For each of us, he is a different person."

"Still, you're the one I am chasing."

"Because you have no choice now!"

"No, because I want to."

"Why do you want to?"

"Because I have no choice."

"Look at the mess you've made! You should be punished for starting it!"

"I didn't start it, you started it!"

"No, you started it!"

"No, you started it!"

"No, you started it!"

"Let's play!"

The two burst into the valley, whose colors started returning, dripping from the sky with the first slim sunbeams. They groped around, splashing prints of green and brown, sliding down the hills, skipping over the heaps scattered about. The two attacked the heaps without hesitation, shaking heads, moving arms, bending legs. They talked and laughed, trying to breathe life into lifeless bodies. They ran from one to the other in widening circles, Hatti after Skolla, Skolla after Hatti, their dark hair flapping in the strengthening wind. They ran and ran and turned and turned, laughing and growling intermittently.

"Let's play!" echoed the hills cheerfully.

"Let's play!" shrieked the voices of the two as they stood one in front of the other among the bodies, among the hills, among the two armies on top of them, among the recurring time, and among the blowing invisible wind.

MAGIC DAYS

They were sitting on colorful cube-shaped pillows: a few were orange, some were purple, some turquoise. One quavered with each sound or movement like grape jello trying to absorb stimuli, some rotated in coordination with the movements of their guests, two or three cube-pillows seemed to incline to the left and then right in turn; the sitters slid off the surface, so slippery they were. Whether they were made of fabric, as suggested by their mysterious inner warmth, silicon, as suggested by the way the rays bounced off their shiny corners, sponge, as the countless drops of water landing on them soaked so quickly, or whether they were simply the fruits of someone's wild imagination, growing in the middle of the forest after a dream just like mushrooms appear after a brief summer storm, was impossible to tell. Mostly because none of the figures present at this little gathering really seemed to care.

Encircled by the woods, they were hidden from the outer world. Deep amongst the large trunks that like pillars supported the azure sky, soft moss covered the wet white rocks that accumulated by the river banks like marbles. Ferns stretched to tickle the ankles of the seated guests, sticking to their soles like chameleon feet. The cool splash of the transparent water running by filled the valley and the guests' minds subtly.

"You know," said the fair-headed boy who was sitting on a pistachio-colored pillow, "the woods are not as quiet as they seem to be."

Hemi, the golden half-cat, blinked slowly in agreement. Her

short tail jerked and she hid her two paws underneath her glossy fur.

"But still, it is calm here," replied the turtle slowly, "calm. It's one of those words that quickly lose their meaning, though. Calm. Calm. Calm. What is it even supposed to describe?"

"Peaceful, quiet, and without worry, according to the dictionary," peeped the squirrel, squeezing the definition between the last and current bite while still chewing the addictive coffee bean in his tiny paws.

"Why should it be calm? Talk and chatter are supposed to be lively," said the red-headed girl, crossing her legs so that her skirt no longer hid the ruby of her pillow, "let's talk."

"Right," the fair-headed boy interfered again, "let's talk."

"Very well," agreed a fairy, her lime complexion glistening under the bright sun. She waved her butterfly wings a little before folding them again. "Let's talk of fairytales."

"No fairytales!" exclaimed a gentle bird with delicate paper fans for wings, "Don't you see she suggested that because she *is* a fairy? That's just selfish. Let's read fanfiction."

"Stop it, you two," cried a girl in a fuchsia shirt, tying her blond curls with a rubber band so that they wouldn't fall into her pale face, "I will speak. I'll tell you something that really happened to me. Something that I have never told anyone before."

"Then why are you telling this now?" questioned Hemi, winking whimsically.

"Aren't we all a little weird?" replied the girl. After a short pause, during which everyone's anticipation galloped toward her pillow and sat down comfortably, she began in a low voice.

***

"She stared into those black eyes and she cried and cried and cried. How could it happen? How could the one thing in the world that she truly loved, that kept her alive, that vibrated every nerve in her body with hot anticipation, cease to exist for her?

'Why?' she asked, but her voice was stifled by the suffocating tears barricading her throat, closing on her soul.

'There is no time,' was the answer. Cold and simple. It pierced her last hope like a sword piercing a young heart.

Sobbing, she turned around and ran. She ran through the long hallways, hardly able to perceive her numb senses through the watery mist in her eyes. Her steps were nothing more than an echo, reaching her from far, dead cliffs, the smell of lavender and mothballs in the air was no more than a faint drop of old perfume mixed with dust. The bright colors of the tapestries all outstretched their watery fibers, reaching into one another, mingling and mixing until everything turned pitch black. And she cried and fell deeper and deeper into that darkness.

Strange memories suddenly occupied her mind, now that she gave up control over it, lighting her insides like an ancient film lighting faintly too big a canvas. She remembered warm sand between her toes, scratching and tickling as it cut into her skin, extremely sensitive while trapped in the odd memory. Waves of green and white crashed on the sharp beach rocks, even though they were all smaller than her fingernails. She shivered as she felt the salty drops pinching her arms again and again. For a moment or two, she let her eyelids cover her vision. The lashes weaved into each other easily, like obedient strings of silk. When she opened her eyes again, the sky was gone, hidden behind an enormous shape. She could see only the bow of the ship, stretching over the horizon. The hull rubbed against the sharp pebbles, motionless, waiting. Only now did the air tremble with noise. It was the noise of children, talking and yelling and laughing. They poured over the deck like a bubbling cocktail, jumping on the sand and running, dancing away. One was separated from the crowd as it fell. She shrieked. He fell and was caught, laughing, before hitting the sharp rocks by the water that was unnaturally clear, practically invisible to the human eye.

She kept running through the hallway, entering every room, not skipping a single door. There was the blue room and the red room and the pink room and the yellow room, and more and more, but, to her, they all seemed colorless. Her confused mind recalled the colors automatically from some code burned into it because of the number of times she had entered those chambers in the past."

***

The words lowered into a whisper that dissembled gradually but did not disappear. The quiet mystery of the continuation hung suspended in the air. At last the listeners moved, jerking their heads and legs as if shaking off a sleepy cold.

Few mouthed the words "I'm sorry" in mute sympathy without demanding an explanation for this confused story, for great griefs are often unexplainable.

"The sand between the toes..." muttered someone,

digesting the vision.

"Once, I hit my toes on a beach like that," a curly imp attempted to untangle the tension, "chasing a dog. My toes still hurt," he drifted in a dreamy voice. The fuchsia girl tried to say something but he went on. "Toes are strange. Always ugly. So jointless. They are bound to get hit." The imp stretched his bare legs, examining the subject of his monologue. "I don't like toes. My toes still hurt. I like toads. I don't know why so many people don't. Jordo the toad. Cute, cute, cute. So Jordo. He is a good toad. He is slimy but he jumps really well. I'm glad he never made me remember his Latin name. If he did, I most probably wouldn't. And I also wouldn't have liked him, that's for sure. But he is hurting right now. Just like my toes. Because all we have to do is change a few letters… and we'd have toads on our feet. Ribbit." He giggled. "I would make a pretty good toad. It must be fun to jump like them. But nobody beats Jordo. He's very toadish."

"Oh, you don't know what you're talking about!" croaked the bulgy animal sitting right next to him, a toad that remained unnoticed until that very moment, insulted.

This comment was followed by awkward silence.

"Let me tell my story," said someone at last, "I hope it doesn't fall short of yours. It is similar in a way, I dare say."

***

"We were on a trip. We had no time to plan beforehand and would not waste exchanged money on a map, and so we just went where our legs took us. That day it was a park. The neatly cut grass outstretched as far as the eye could see, interrupted only by occasional gravel paths that wound around the randomly placed trees and bushes. The species seemed random as well: a shrub speckled by miniature yellow blossoms hunched beside a young tree whose green and yellow crown seemed too heavy for the trunk that was as thin as a harpist's finger. We walked slowly yet steadily, enjoying the green atmosphere without bothering to bury ourselves in the details of every plant, only sucking in their visible grace. Some of the tallest trees were connected by a wire that skipped from one to the other, touching the branches gently before moving on, leaving a black strip as a trail. We looked up, to follow the electric trail above us, noticing an occasional forgotten Christmas ornament swaying in the April breeze. As our sights reached the third or fourth branch, we noticed a movement between the bright leaves. After an adjustment to the light we understood we were looking at a bird. It was a pigeon or a turtle dove of some sort, its feathers were the color of buttermilk and legs brownish red like rust. The creature moved to and fro, raising its wings every now and then to straighten the feathers. For some reason, we could not keep walking. There was something strange about the bird. We examined it for a long time, unable to put our fingers on it. After a significant waste of time we gave up and cast one last glance at the pigeon before moving along. Then we saw it. The creature's striped neck was thinner than usual split in two. The two necks supported two bird heads gazing back at us with four empty, orange eyes.

We gasped, nearly choking with horrified surprise, turned rapidly around and quickly walked away, trying to leave the disturbing sight behind. Yet now that we had noticed that bird, we started noticing more and more. There were turtle pigeons on the bushes, on the wires, on the fountains, all white and clean, all two headed. Unwillingly, we felt our puzzled fear of the strange phenomenon grow inside us, dripping slowly into our intestines like sticky syrup. It made us sick, it made us weak. We hurried our steps, our hearts started pounding, and we leaned forward, using all our weight against the strengthening wind pushing us back. We were running through the park that seemed to stretch more and more, always several meters before us, not allowing escape. Oddly, we were the only ones distraught by the creatures; passersby lingered here and there, watching us with their slow eyes dully. Maybe they were entirely used to birds having two heads instead of one, maybe this was how birds were in this place. Maybe no one except us noticed the extra head at all. Or maybe, maybe, we only imagined this strange deformity in a moment of frenzy, and it didn't exist at all. But every time this thought crossed our minds we would look at another bird and see it as the others before, clear as day.

Panting desperately, we finally escaped the lawns and found ourselves in a narrow lane with renaissance buildings on either side. The atmosphere here was different, as if a giant bluish curtain had been drawn from the sky. We bent our knees and leaned on them, trying to catch our breath. The fear clogging us gradually faded, but we didn't allow ourselves much time. Upon standing straight again, we noticed that the heavy oak door of the nearest blue house was open. Without much thought, we entered. A steep wooden staircase climbed to the first floor, not allowing entrance to the ground floor, if there indeed was one. We followed it, our shoulders touching the picture-laden walls. A soft fuzzy carpet welcomed us and, soothed, we went on. Turning right with the corridor, we encountered another oak door, open as well. Behind it, however, the floor ended, creating a sort of chasm above a pool of water. A boat floated down there, advancing slowly in our direction. When it was close enough, we could spot a long dining table carrying trays and silverware surrounded by soft Louis XIV chairs. All were empty, except for one at the head of the table, upon which sat a fine figure clothed in a long satin dress.

'Come dine with us, honorable guests,' the lady from the boat addressed us, 'you must calm down and rest.'

A tranquil feeling accompanied her clear voice, making the horrors of the park seem like a nearly forgotten dream. We jumped through the door, expecting to land on the deck at any moment."

***

Unlike that of the fuchsia girl's, this ending was unpredicted. It simply took over the story, a blank page covering the black and white lines. It took a few seconds for everyone to understand the speaker had finished.

"And?" the coy question followed.

"And what?" replied the speaker, as if forgetting his speech entirely.

The toad next to the imp blinked. "Do you have anything to add?" she addressed him snarkily.

"Impossible."

"I had dinner on a boat once," said a beaver dreamily, "it didn't last very long. We all fell into the water. It was cold, refreshing. I guess I ate too much that day."

"Yes, everyone could use a swim." replied the angelfish, whose voice was somewhat distorted because of the fishbowl. With every breath she released a miniature tornado of bubbles that later clung to the surface like glass beads.

"Not everyone can," someone protested.

"Of course everyone can. Not everything is possible, but swimming always is," said the angelfish confidently. "You can swim in rivers, lakes, seas, and oceans. You can swim in Europe, Asia, America, every part of this world. You can swim in other worlds, wherever life exists, because, as everyone knows, life means water. But you don't necessarily need water to swim. You can swim in any other liquid. You can swim in outer space. If you try really hard, you can swim in the air."

"Speaking of swimming," spoke a middle-aged man, whose open briefcase displayed a dazzling collection of fragile origami figures, "and thinking of fish, I would like to share my story with you."

***

"You didn't take a vacation. You didn't buy the tickets. And yet, you don't know how, you've found yourself on a plane, expecting to be in the air for the next fourteen hours. Your destination: New Zealand. Why? You don't remember. Where exactly? This slipped your mind. You do know for how long you will be gone, though: four hours, if ignoring the time spent on the plane and in the airport. Overall: fourteen hours there, two additional hours to leave the airport, four hours in the exotic destination, two hours back in the airport, and finally fourteen hours to return. This is a total of 36 hours, or 2160 minutes, which sounds like overwhelmingly little and a terrible lot at the same time.

Perhaps if the destination were different, it would have been enough time for a short trip. Perhaps it was your fault for choosing New Zealand without considering the conditions, if you indeed had a choice. Maybe your company decided to send you to an important meeting, or to attend a valuable lecture. Maybe you planned to treat your family to a vacation but bought the tickets half-asleep, forgetting to check the times and number of tickets purchased. Maybe you won a lottery or a bidding war of some sort, collected enough points for a free flight by traveling or shopping.

You can't remember. But, to be honest, you don't try very hard.

Anyway, be the reason of your trip what it may, you have decided to use your short time wisely, according to your own will. You are determined to see the local natural sights that no other place can be compared to. You wish to see the sapphire blue sky, to feel the blowing wind, to hear the roaring water. You want to lie down on the soft dirt, surrounded by the ants and ladybugs, one with nature, for four hours.

You sit back and look out the oval window, watch the white stripes of clouds float lazily beneath you, spotting the dim shadow of the plane from time to time. You sigh, and your own warm breath lands in your lap, folds into a neat bundle, and purrs quietly, and you feel the vibrations reaching you through your jeans, through your skin, your blood slows, your heart relaxes. Consoled, you close your eyes, breathing in and out…in…and out…in…and out…

When your heavy lids lift again, you are standing, rocking a little to and fro as if caught in a trance, as if slow-dancing to your own music, which is nonexistent or inaudible to the rest of the world. Gravity gently pulls your hair, then the front of your shirt, and, trying to fight it, you start realizing where you are. On a rocky mountaintop. Scarves of fog are hung around you by barely visible strips of cool, glossy, smeared raindrops. Your head lowers to observe the ground, you take a few steps, distinguishing the earthly stone from the heavenly clouds, reaching a round hole, a well, into which poured mighty streams of water appearing from nowhere.

'You must get down,' a voice tells you from behind.

'How?' your voice trembles.

'Fly.' And before you realize it, two strong hands push you, you trip, the ground beneath your feet crumbles, and you hear the wind whistling by your side. You are too scared to shout, and just fall, awaiting the ocean's cold mouth to swallow you.

And suddenly you land on a surface so hard that in spite of the omnipresent chill your side is burnt severely. It is ice: a wide, round sheet of ice about five times the size of the round well above. You raise your sore head and see the circle of white light surrounded by a carpet of plants climbing on the ceiling of the hollow mountain. They cover the rough walls as well, climbing on top of each other, racing toward the light in their plant-speed. Looking down to your bruised self again, you see the thick ice and distinguish splashes of color here and there, floating slowly, disappearing and reappearing like Chinese paper lanterns."

***

From the man's briefcase rose a swarm of fireflies, awakened by the late hour. The rays that found their way into the forest were now low and yellow, like a friendly campfire, and together with the lampyrids' sleepy green, they washed the remains of the day off the ancient trees. "Like Chinese paper lanterns…" he repeated quietly, deep in thought.

"Fish are truly extraordinary creatures," remarked the imp.

The angelfish grinned.

"Yet not as extraordinary as jellyfish," remarked the squirrel hastily, without even noticing the angry eyes leering at him from the fishbowl. "Jellyfish are made of up to 98% water; they are one of the oldest living forms on Earth. Thanks to their biological simplicity they have amazing regeneration skills, and thanks to a color changing pigment they can easily startle predators."

The fairy turned to him. "You know what, why don't you tell us your story?" While talking she cast a questioning glance to the others.

"Yes, I'd be interested to hear it," said the briefcase man politely. Some of the other guests nodded hesitatingly, not really knowing whether to agree but reluctant to be left out of the conversation.

"Very well," chirped the squirrel and let go of the coffee bean he had been nibbling the entire time. A dim *bang* was heard when the hard, round bean hit the soft forest ground.

***

"They arrived around midday. Stepping out of the bus, with more heavy bags than their hands could carry, they realized that they could have taken the later ride. It was too late to go for a trip and too early to stay in the room. They didn't think there wouldn't be a need to check in. So they stared for a while at the wooden cottage that was supposed to serve as their lodging for the following few days. Apparently, it didn't match the high expectations of experienced travelers. Somewhat suspiciously, they approached the front wall, moving a little to the left as if drawing a large circle with their footprints, like curious cats fearfully sniffing a new piece of furniture. The brass key shone bravely on the wooden background from its hook near the door. They winced at the loud creak it made while opening.

The narrow cottage was furnished with numerous beds standing so closely to one another that they created a sort of platform along the entire left wall. On the opposite wall there was a small opening leading to a tiny room containing a miniature shower and a little toilet, and the only window of the cottage, no bigger than a postcard. And just like a postcard, it was a bright square of vivid color greeting the dark interior from a far magical land, dancing around the frame ever so elegantly, threatening to overflow this border and spill over the wall like a watercolor stain.

They could not open the suitcases on the floor for lack of space, and therefore laid them on the beds in order to unpack. Pants, shorts, T-shirts were unfolded, refolded, and carried to the open cupboard awaiting them a few steps away. But just as they were lowered toward the shelf, the hands holding them slowed, hesitated, and then carried the clothes back to the bed, only to return to the cupboard without them. What stopped the unpacking process was a thick book in soft cover. Each millimeter of each page displayed in the brightest ink a most detailed picture, together creating a collage of grass and seedling, caterpillars and beetles, wrinkles in the barks of mighty trees disappearing into a tangle of branches and leaves and blue bits of sky.

They turned page after page, their eyes trying to soak enough of the wondrous pictures before they were replaced by others, competing with growing curiosity. One page showed a babbling brook sliding into a field of long steel-blue grass, whose bent stems created still waves reflecting the sunlight from above. One unraveled a jungle of violets in all shapes and sizes, hanging from the tall trees like curtains of sparkling amethysts blending into hills of lavender. Another presented rows of platinum ants climbing a stairway of quietly growing rocks surrounded by whispering shadows.

Blinking with effort to absorb all this inexplicable beauty, they closed the book altogether, their head lowering a little as if loaded with too much information. Only then did they notice the plain letters on the cover.

Choose your own forest.

Was this a sort of catalogue offering countless miraculous transformations of the wild nature around? Could these changes indeed occur? What was the meaning of all this? What was such a catalogue doing in a stranded cottage?

Be the answers what they may, they decided to choose.

After long consideration they picked a Japanese garden of sorts. They were enchanted by the slender trees, each standing on perfect half-circle bump, stretching crooked branches upwards like oriental dancers. Some held crowns of green between their wrinkly twigs; some held blossoms of cotton candy. A silver stripe of water spiraled around the low hills and zigzagged by the young bonsai-like bushes.

They stared at the image, attempting to engrave every detail into their memory, focusing all their will on the picture. Then, eyes closed with concentration, they groped their way out of the cottage and with a gentle smile, felt the wind caressing their face. Once more they visualized the delicate earrings of cherries and pink and white leaf confetti before looking around.

Nothing changed.

Somewhat disappointed they sighed, and slowly started wandering about, letting their tired sight fly from one plant to another without paying attention.

Suddenly a memory in their mind blinked, shining from the tiredness like a lit beacon. They turned around, searching for the object that awoke this memory. It was a group of crystal pink leaves, round like pearls and thin like coins. The resemblance to the leaves in the picture was obvious, even without the hills and slender trees. After a short while their attention was drawn to a ripe cherry dangling from above. Gradually, they noticed more and more details similar to their chosen forest: bent twigs, strings of silver on the ground, pink blossoms here and there. Delighted and amused, they wandered with ease, enjoying the beauty all around. They realized that by choosing the forest of their dreams and looking for it within reality they started perceiving the wonders of the woods, however small and insignificant. They crouched by a river hurrying to pass. They withdrew their hands from their pockets, finishing out a miniature boat in a bottle. With a smile, they placed the boat on the back of a miniature wave and watched as it was taken away by the current."

***

Night had joined the guests and nestled up on the cube pillows, in the folds of their clothes, against the tall trees. People and fairies and animals and imps started feeling the night inside their tired thoughts.

"What a day…" yawned Hemi the half-cat.

"What a magical day."

"Just like the ones we'd heard of," smiled the girl in the fuchsia shirt.

"We still have all night, though," remarked the fair-headed boy, "why don't you share your story?" He turned toward me.

***

"I fell asleep… I await my awakening."

ACKNOWLEDGMENTS

The stories in this collection formed my path. They helped me navigate through the hollow blackness and safely find a ray of light to hold on to. Cinnabar Nocturne had been my most liberating, enjoyable project so far, and nothing I had ever written before has ever felt as right.

I'd like to thank my grandmother and Mamu, who initiated the process and made me fight for what's really important.

Thank you, Ervin, for being my role model and a source of inspiration all these years. Special thanks to Natálka Musilová, for her superpower to always find the bright side of…well, everything. I thank my parents and my sister for the support, the love, and of course for Sesqui.

I thank Fritz Rickhoff for the amazing and honest feedback, my editor Jennifer Paul for doing a wonderful job and for the helpful comments. Her website https://makinggoodstories.wordpress.com was of great help. I also thank Richard Pinard, Agáta Motlochová and Kačka Matějovcová for the encouragement.

Cinnabar Nocturne is composed of very personal stories, but I think it is worth sharing. I hope that you will enjoy this book too, and that you will find a reflection of yourself in my stories.

Tiana Or-Gordon, December 2019